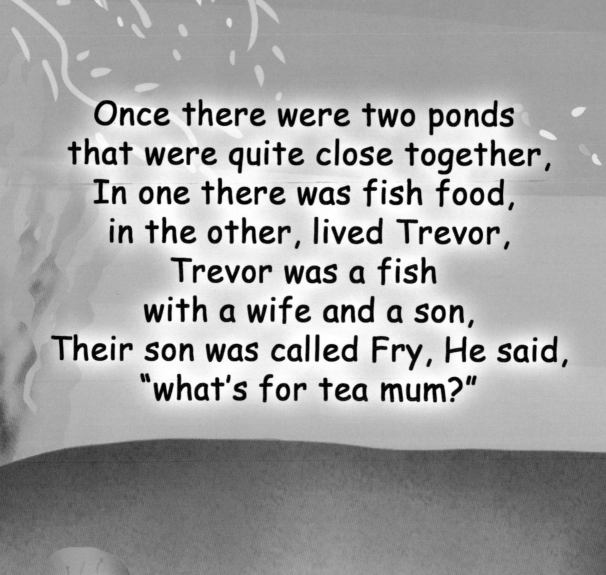

Once there were two ponds
that were quite close together,
In one there was fish food,
in the other, lived Trevor,
Trevor was a fish
with a wife and a son,
Their son was called Fry, He said,
"what's for tea mum?"

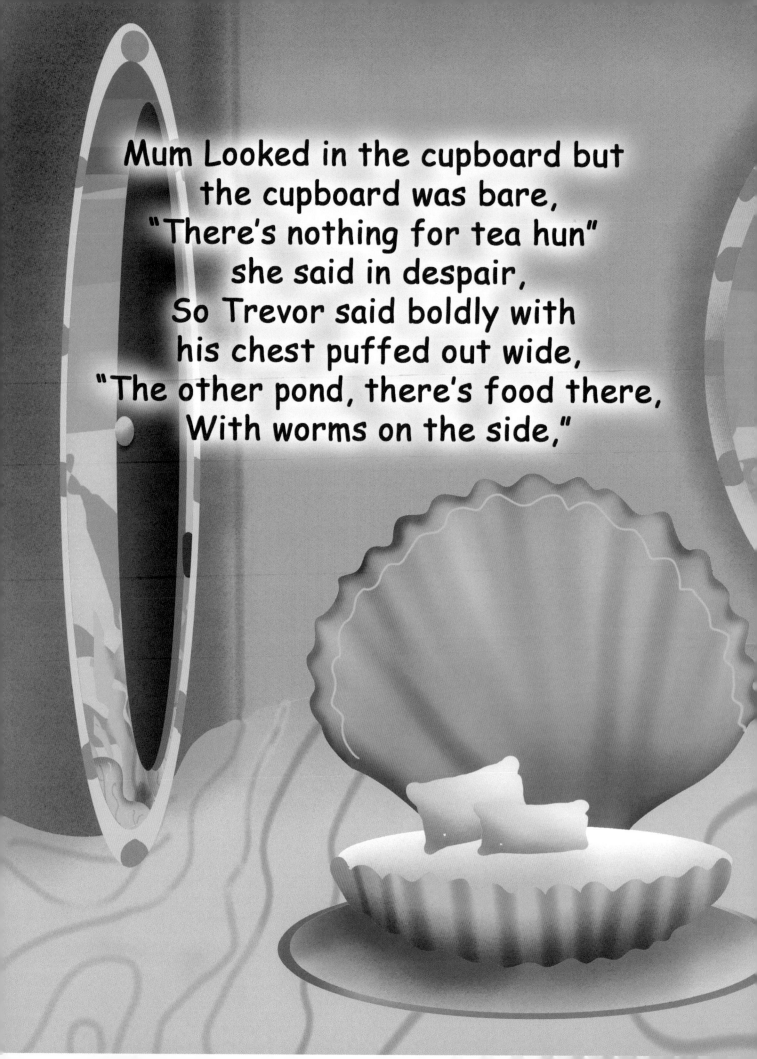

Mum Looked in the cupboard but
the cupboard was bare,
"There's nothing for tea hun"
she said in despair,
So Trevor said boldly with
his chest puffed out wide,
"The other pond, there's food there,
With worms on the side,"

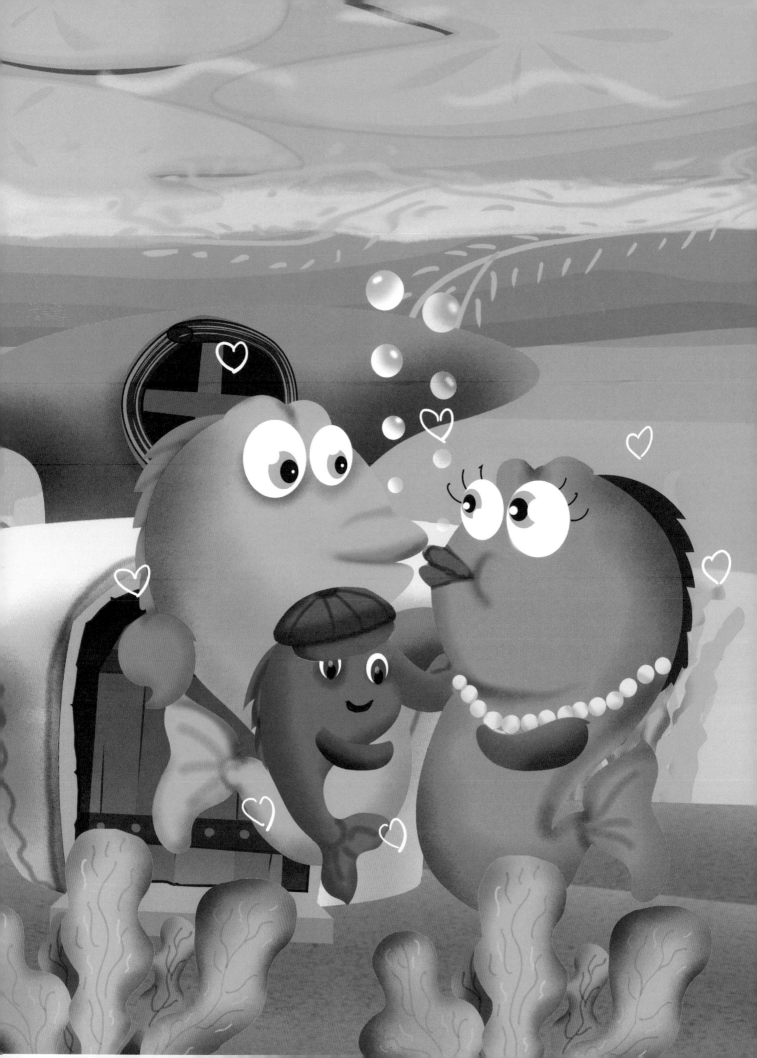

"You can't get there" said mum,
"You'll never make it" said Fry,
"Just watch me" said Trevor,
As he kissed them goodbye,

As Trevor set off through a sunken farm trough, He passed his friend Bill who asked "*Where you off?*" Trevor told him his plan and Bill howled with laughter,"You can't walk on land Trev, I think you get dafter".

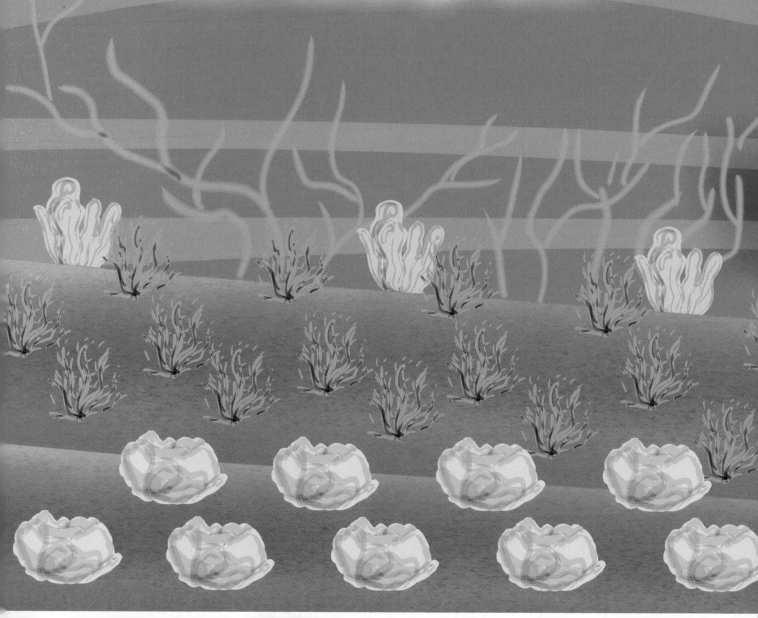

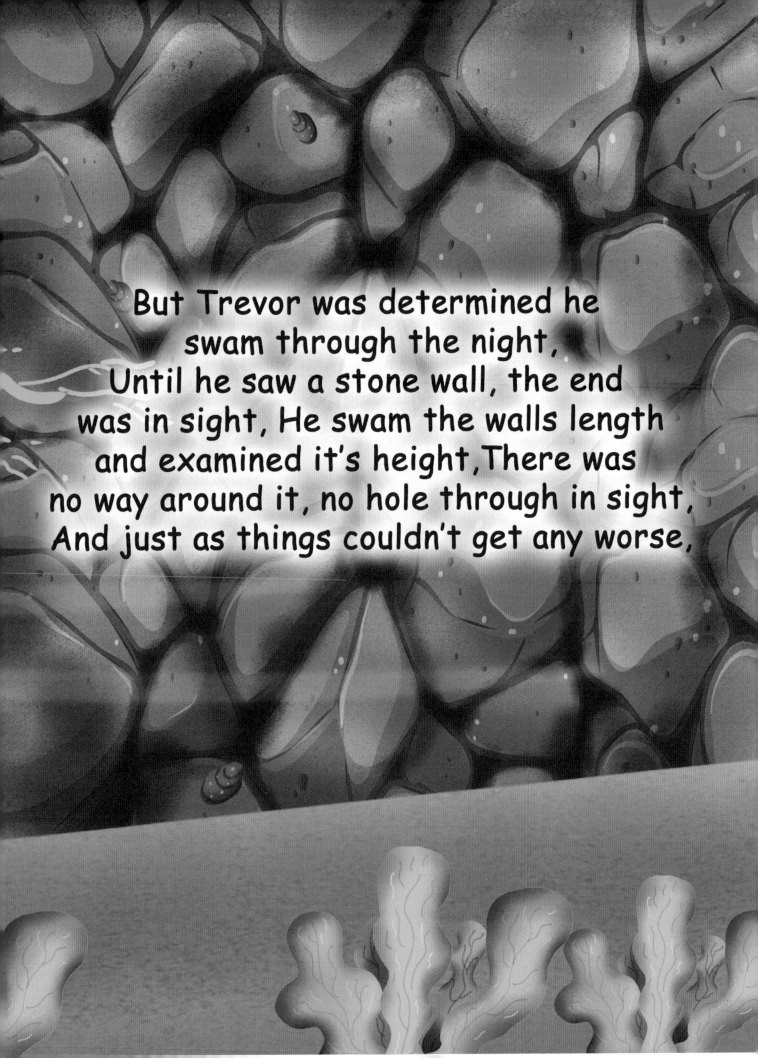

But Trevor was determined he
swam through the night,
Until he saw a stone wall, the end
was in sight, He swam the walls length
and examined it's height,There was
no way around it, no hole through in sight,
And just as things couldn't get any worse,

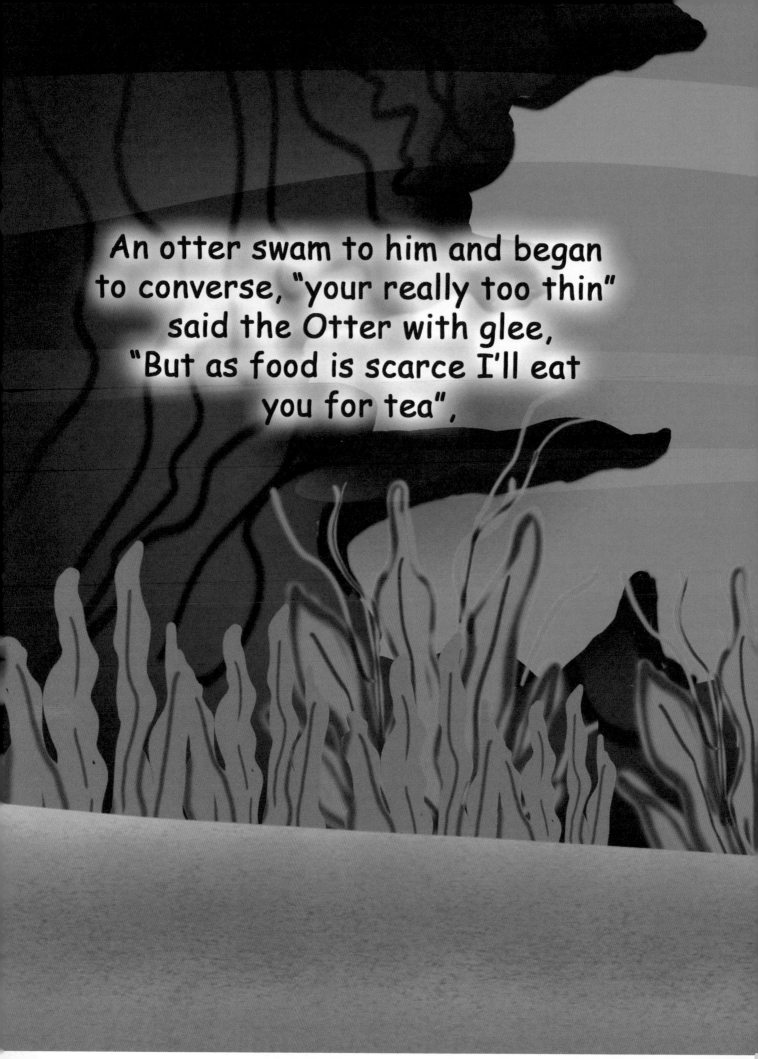

"why me?" bellowed Trevor
"there's food through that wall",
"There's fish food, there's insects,
there's food for us all",
"Is that right?" said the otter
"let's have a look",
And he picked out a stone
with an old fishing hook,

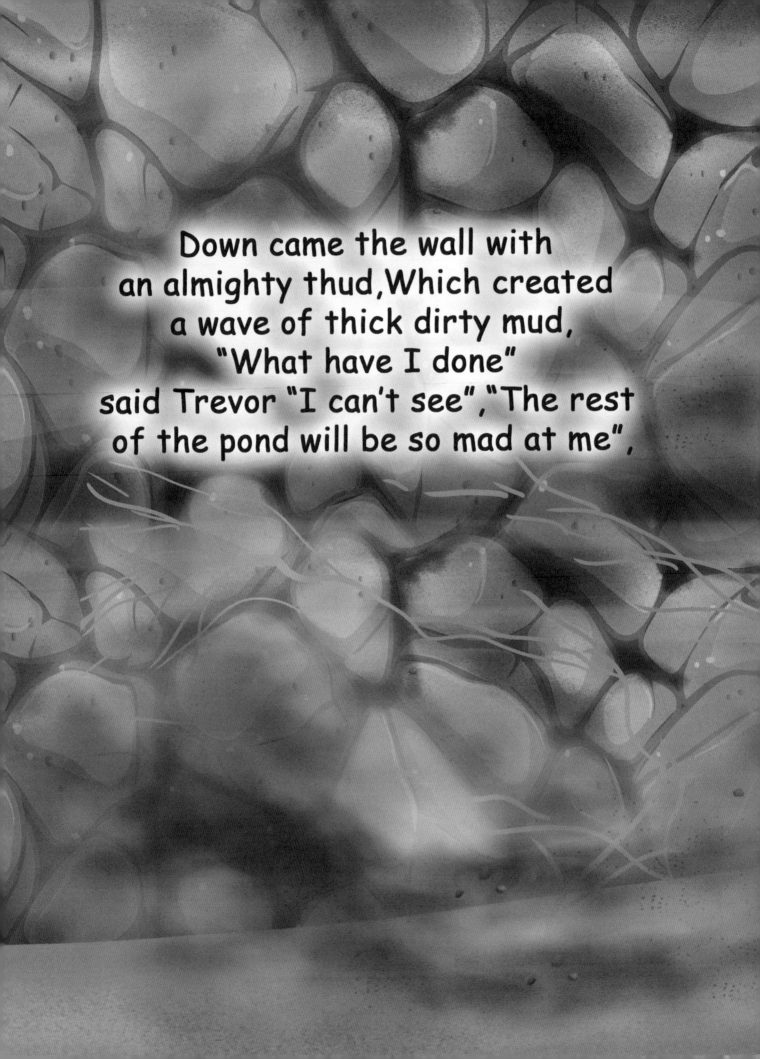

Down came the wall with
an almighty thud,Which created
a wave of thick dirty mud,
"What have I done"
said Trevor "I can't see","The rest
of the pond will be so mad at me",

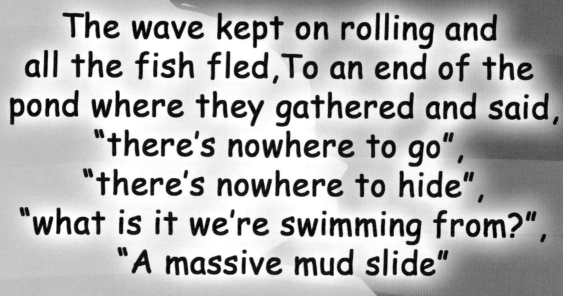

The wave kept on rolling and
all the fish fled,To an end of the
pond where they gathered and said,
"there's nowhere to go",
"there's nowhere to hide",
"what is it we're swimming from?",
"A massive mud slide"

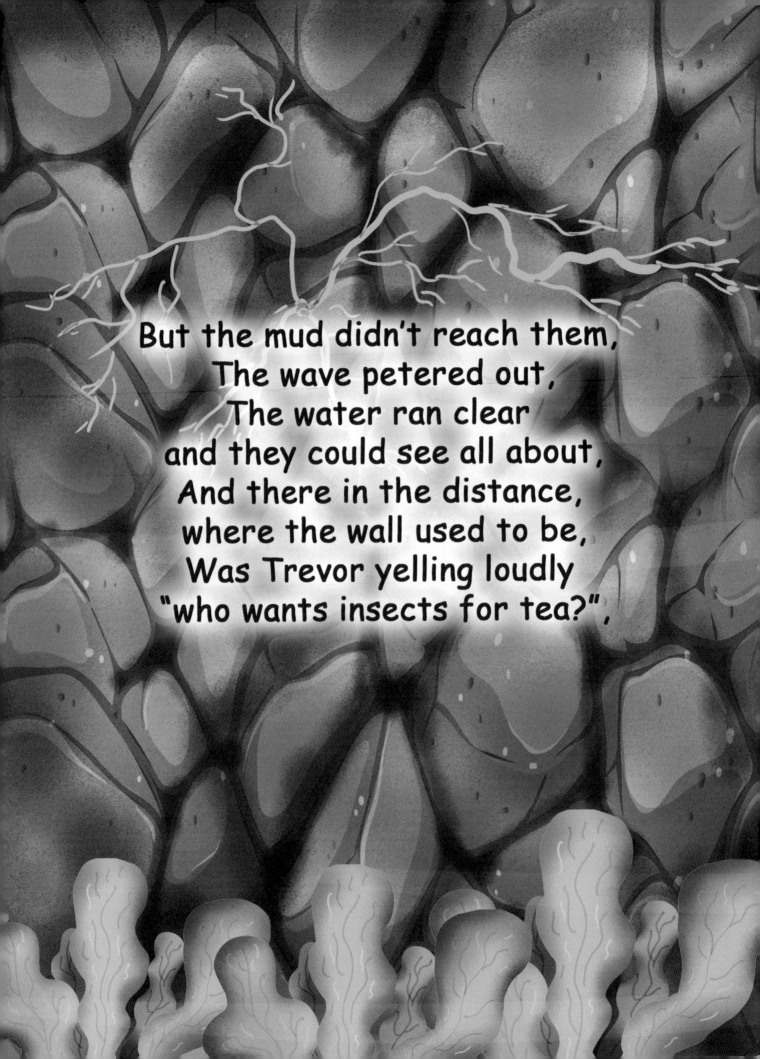

But the mud didn't reach them,
The wave petered out,
The water ran clear
and they could see all about,
And there in the distance,
where the wall used to be,
Was Trevor yelling loudly
"who wants insects for tea?",

They all sped across
in Trevor's direction,
Through to a pond with a diverse
selection Of freshwater mussels
and insects a plenty,

Trevor's wife took his fin and
kissed his cheek gently, "I'm sorry"
said Trevor "it didn't go as I planned".
"I got an Otter to help me,
I needed a hand"

Fry swam around singing
"my dad's a hero,
Last night we'd no food and now worms
by the kilo",So two ponds are now
one due to one little fish,

Who made his friends happy
and the otter's O.K....ish,

Printed in Great Britain
by Amazon